Roger Hurn used to be an actor in 'The Exploding Trouser Company'. He has also appeared on 'The Weakest Link' on TV – and he won!

Now he spends his time writing and telling stories. His scariest and spookiest experience came when he went to an old ghost town in the Wild West of the USA. This gave him the idea for **Spook Squad.**

He hopes you enjoy reading the Spook Squad's adventures as much as he enjoyed writing them.

Spook Squad
Things That Go Bump in the Night
by Roger Hurn
Illustrated by Peter Richardson

Published by Ransom Publishing Ltd.
Radley House, 8 St. Cross Road, Winchester, Hampshire
SO23 9HX, UK
www.ransom.co.uk

ISBN   978 184167 075 1
First published in 2012

Things That Go Bump in the Night

by Roger Hurn

Ransom

Dead End Junction

The Ghost Train Railway

Ghouls' Graveyard

It's the dead centre of Otherworld!

Vlad the Bad's Castle

The Isle of Fright

The Wraith Pits

They really are the pits!

The Haunted Pyramid

Your mummy warned you about this place

Here There Be Dragons

Banshee Bay

Where the wind never stops howling!

They sleep in the day and fight knights!

Otherworld

GOBLIN GULCH
The home of
messy eaters

FANG MOUNTAINS
You'll say 'Fangs for
nothing' if you try to
climb them

**KRAKEN
LAKE**

Swim at
your
own risk!

SPOOK CITY

THE ZOMBI RIVER

WEREWOLF WOODS
Avoid when the
moon is full!

Otherworld

Where is Otherworld?

The far side of a shadow.

Who lives there?

Ghouls, ghosts, long-leggedy beasties and things that go bump in the night.

Why do the creatures who live there come to our world?

To make mischief.

6

Rhee the Banshee answers readers' questions.

How do they get here?

> They slip through secret gateways
> when you're not looking.

Can humans go to Otherworld?

> Yes, but they shouldn't.

Why not?

> Because they never come back.

Why not?

> Trust me – you really
> **DO NOT** want to know!

Meet The SPOOK SQUAD

Emma

FYI: She spends her life getting hold of the wrong end of the stick.

Loves: Getting the point.

Hates: Muddy sticks.

Fact: She doesn't like vampires – she thinks they're a pain in the neck.

Roxy

FYI: Don't call her 'Ginger' – unless you want to eat your dinner through a straw.

Loves: Being a strawberry blonde.

Hates: Seeing red.

Fact: She reckons cannibal goblins are messy eaters, so she won't be joining their fang club.

Nita

FYI: This girl gets gadgets. Give her a paper clip, a rubber band, a tin can and an A4 battery and she'll rig up a gizmo that'll blow your gran's pop socks off.

Loves: Fixing things.

Hates: Fixing it – if it ain't broke.

Fact: Nita has invented ghost-proof wheels for her bike. They don't have any spooks!

Leena

FYI: If she was any sharper you could use her to slice bread.

Loves: Big words.

Hates: Small minds.

Fact: She prefers whatwolves and whenwolves to werewolves.

Aunt Rhee

FYI: Rhee's not the kind of aunt who gives you a woolly jumper for Christmas.

Loves: Walking on the wild side.

Hates: Things that go bump in the night.

Fact: Rhee is just too cool for ghouls.

Rattle

FYI: Rattle says he's a poltergeist. He thinks poltergeists are posher than ghosts.

Loves: Boo-berry pie and I-scream.

Hates: People who sneak up behind him and shout BOO!

Fact: Rattle's only happy when he's moaning.

Interview with Roxy

The Spook Squad's Roxy answers readers' questions.

Is Rhee really your auntie?

> No, she's a friend of my mum's. I've known her forever but I didn't know she was a banshee. How cool is that?

Do you like being in the Spook Squad?

> Yes, but it can be a bit scary.

Which is worse – a zombie or a vampire?

> Neither. I think they're both dead even.

Who is your best friend in the Spook Squad?

> Today it's Nita because she shared her chocolate bar with me – but I really like them all. We've been friends since nursery school.

Which is your favourite Spook Squad adventure?

> The Scream Team.

Why?

> Because we beat The Scream Team without any help from Rhee!

The Hobgoblin

Description: He's sneaky, freaky and creepy!

Strength: He has light fingers.

Weakness: If he hurts his leg he turns into a hobblin' goblin!

Likes: People who leave their keys in the door and their windows open.

Dislikes: Being called a 'tea leaf'.

Don't say: 'You've got an honest face.'

Scream Scale Rating: You'll be the one screaming if he steals something from you!

Chapter One

Lights in the Sky

Rhee and Rattle were watching a late night TV horror movie about a monster with no neck. The film was at a really scary bit when suddenly they heard a very loud knocking on the door of the Old Tower.

'Arggghhh! It's the Lost Neck Monster. He's come looking for his neck!' wailed Rattle. He dived behind the armchair.

Rhee grabbed a sharp stake and then

tip-toed across the room. She peeked through the spy hole. She sighed with relief and unlocked the door. The Spook Squad tumbled in, all talking at once.

Rhee held up her hands. 'Hey, I've only got one pair of ears,' she said. 'So can just one of you tell me what's up?'

'We've seen some lights in the sky,' said Roxy.

'Huh, is that all?' moaned Rattle, as he flew up from behind the chair. 'I've got news for you lot. Those lights in the sky are called stars.'

'Duh! We know that,' said Nita. 'But these lights weren't stars. They kept moving about like sudden bursts of flame.'

Rhee raised her eyebrows. 'Hmm … that

is odd,' she said.

Suddenly the room shook, as something heavy landed with a bump somewhere outside in the darkness.

Rattle dived back behind the armchair. The Spook Squad stared at each other open-mouthed.

Bump! The room shook again.

'What the heck was that?' said Roxy.

Bump!

'I don't know,' said Rhee. 'But let's find out!'

Chapter Two

Things That Go Bump in the Night

The banshee and the Spook Squad dashed out of the Old Tower and came face-to-face with two dragons. The dragons were thumping their tails down hard on the ground. Smoke poured out from their jaws.

'Hey,' said Nita, 'Don't you dragons know that smoking is bad for your health?'

The largest dragon opened its mouth

wide. Flames flickered in its throat.

'Uh oh! And there's no smoke without fire!' shouted Leena.

'Duck!' yelled Roxy. 'It's going to barbecue us!'

The Spook Squad hit the deck. But the dragon didn't spit flame at them.

'Hello, Rhee,' it said. 'Sorry about all the thumping. But our claws are too big for your door knocker.'

The Spook Squad picked themselves up again. They grinned sheepishly at the dragons. The dragons ignored them.

Rhee looked at the girls. She shook her head and sighed. Then she turned to face the dragons.

'Hello Grak, Hello Grik,' she said. 'What are you two doing here?'

Grik, the smaller dragon, answered. 'Oh Rhee, a thief has stolen an egg from our den.'

'Yes,' growled Grak. Its voice was like two jagged rocks rubbing together. 'So we need your help to track down the thief and get our egg back, before it hatches.'

Rhee nodded. 'You've got it,' she said.

Rhee leapt onto Grak's back. The huge dragon flapped its wings and rose up into the air. Grik followed him.

'Hey, what about us?' yelled Leena.

Rhee looked down at the Spook Squad. 'You lot can just chill out. I'm off to Otherworld with Grak and Grik to make

life hot for the egg thief,' she said.

Then Rhee and the two dragons soared off up into the night sky.

Chapter Three

Lotsa Loot

'Oh those poor dragons,' said Emma. 'Why would anybody want to steal their egg?'

'I don't know,' said Roxy. 'All I know is Rhee's left us behind – again!'

'Yeah,' said Leena. 'We're going to miss out on all the fun – again!'

'Be thankful you are,' said Rattle. 'Dragons are dangerous. And anyone who steals their eggs must be mad.'

'Not mad,' said Nita. 'Just greedy.' Nita held up a copy of the local newspaper. The headline said: *Loot Buys Museum*.

'Listen to this,' she said. 'Lotsa Loot, the world's richest man, has bought the *Strange Stuff* museum.'

'Hey, that museum is right here in our town!' exclaimed Roxy.

'That right, said Nita. 'Well, Mr Loot wants strange things to put in his museum. He's offering to pay a fortune to anyone who brings him something really weird.'

Leena clicked her fingers. 'And a dragon's egg would be just what he's looking for.'

'But a dragon's egg must be worth millions!' said Emma.

'That's true,' said Roxy, 'but Lotsa Loot is a billionaire, so he can afford to buy it.'

'I bet the thief is at the museum right now, selling the egg to Mr Loot,' said Nita.

'But surely Mr Loot won't buy a stolen egg?' said Emma.

A horrible, cackling laugh filled the air. Rattle pointed a ghostly finger at the Spook Squad.

'Lotsa Loot isn't just the world's richest man – he's also the world's most evil man! He won't care that the dragon egg is stolen.'

'That's terrible,' said Emma.

'Yes, it is,' agreed the little poltergeist.

'But we'll stop him,' said Roxy.

'No you won't,' said Rattle. 'Lotsa Loot is far too mean and scary for you girls to deal with on your own.'

'You think so?' said Leena.

'I do,' said Rattle firmly. Then he puffed himself up. 'But *I* could deal with him, of course.'

'Well, come on then,' said Roxy. 'Let's do it!'

Rattle gulped and turned even whiter than usual. 'Er … I've a better idea,' he said. 'You girls wait here while I go and fetch Rhee back from Otherworld.'

Rattle vanished with a *POP!*

'Oh well,' sighed Emma. 'I guess we had better do as Rattle says.'

The other girls looked at her in horror. 'You must be joking, Em,' said Roxy.

'No way are we staying here,' said Leena. 'We're going where the *eggs*-citement is.'

'We've got an egg thief to catch – and that's no *yolk*,' said Nita.

'*Eggs*-actly!' said Roxy.

'Alright,' said Emma, 'but I just hope we don't end up with egg on our faces.'

Chapter Four

Don't Count Your Dragons Before They Hatch

The *Strange Stuff* museum was a creepy place. It stood in an overgrown garden full of trees and tangled bushes. A light shone out of a ground-floor window.

The Spook Squad crept up to it. Nita peeked through the glass.

'What can you see, Neet?' whispered Roxy.

'Lotsa Loot sitting at a desk with a big

pile of gold coins in front of him,' replied Nita.

Roxy couldn't resist having a look for herself. 'Wow, all that gold must be to pay for the dragon's egg,' she said.

'Right, but there's no sign of the thief,' said Nita, as she leaned forward to take a closer look.

'Ow!' Nita bumped her head on the window. Lotsa Loot glanced up. Roxy and Nita ducked back down out of sight.

'Phew, that was a close call,' muttered Nita, rubbing her head.

'Yeah, you nearly gave Lotsa Loot a heads-up there,' said Roxy.

'Never mind Mr Loot,' said Emma. 'What we need is a heads-up on where the thief is.'

'He must still be on his way here,' said Nita.

'So let's hide behind a tree, and then jump out and grab him as soon as he arrives!' said Roxy.

'But the egg might get broken if there's any rough stuff,' protested Emma.

'Hmm … good point, Em,' said Leena. 'But what else can we do?'

'Nothing,' said Nita. 'So let's just be careful – 'cos I don't want to have to tell two angry dragons that we scrambled their egg!'

No sooner had the Spook Squad hidden themselves when a hobgoblin came sneaking across the garden. He stopped and pulled a large egg out from a pocket in his cloak. He

looked around and then hid the egg
underneath a bush. Then he walked up to
the front door of the museum.

'Grab him, Spook Squad!' hissed Roxy.

'No wait!' said Nita. 'Let him go. We can take the egg while he's inside.'

The door opened and the hobgoblin went into the museum.

The Spook Squad dashed across to the bush and Emma carefully picked up the dragon egg.

'We did it!' exclaimed Roxy. 'We saved the egg!'

'But why did the thief hide the egg out here?' asked Emma.

'Cos he wants the gold before he hands over the egg,' said Leena.

'Remember, Lotsa Loot is evil,' said Roxy. 'So I guess the thief figures that Loot

will try and trick him.'

'But this way, Loot has no choice but to give the thief the gold,' said Nita. 'Otherwise the thief won't tell him where the egg is hidden. Clever, eh?'

'Very clever,' said a cold, cruel voice. 'Now hand me that egg. It's mine!'

The Spook Squad spun round. Lotsa Loot and the hobgoblin were standing right behind them!

Chapter Five

Everything Heats Up

The Spook Squad began to back away slowly.

Lotsa Loot snarled. 'I said, give me my egg!'

He made a grab for it. Emma threw it to Roxy. 'Catch,' she yelled.

Roxy did.

'Don't just stand there,' Loot yelled at the

hobgoblin. 'Get that egg and I'll pay you double!'

The hobgoblin flung himself at Roxy. Roxy sidestepped him and tossed the egg to Leena.

Loot hurled himself at Leena. She dodged him and lobbed the egg to Nita.

Lotsa Loot was furious. 'Right!' he screamed. 'This ends now!'

'It sure does!' shouted a voice from above their heads. Lotsa Loot and the hobgoblin looked up to see two angry dragons and a banshee swooping down on them.

'Arggghhh!' they screamed, as Grak and Grik grabbed them and swept them up into the night sky.

The dragons were silhouetted against the full moon as the two bad guys dangled from the dragons' claws by the seat of their pants.

'Hey,' said Leena, 'that brings a whole new meaning to the word *mooning*!'

Suddenly, Rattle appeared with a 'pop'. 'Well done, Spook Squad,' he said.

'But where is Rhee taking Mr Loot and the thief?' asked Emma.

'Back to Otherworld,' said Rattle. 'Kidnapping dragon eggs is a bad idea – it makes dragons very upset.'

'So what's going to happen?' said Roxy.

Rattle shrugged. 'Things are going to get a bit hot for Mr Loot and the hobgoblin, I'm afraid.'

The Spook Squad gasped and looked horrified.

'Oh don't worry,' he said. 'Everyone will cool down in the end.'

Rattle grinned at the Spook Squad. 'Now, let's get that egg home. You girls can take turns in sitting on it to keep it warm until its mum and dad come back for it!'

'No way!' chorused Emma, Nita, Leena and Roxy.

'Well, what else did you *eggs*-pect?' cackled Rattle. Then he disappeared before the girls could tell him *eggs*-actly where he could put the dragon egg!

The next Spook Squad adventure is

The Scream Team

It's a Scream!

Spook Squad's Scary Joke Page

How do you stop a werewolf chasing you?

Throw a stick and say fetch!

What's got six legs and flies?

A witch giving her cat a ride on her broomstick!

Why was the werewolf arrested at the butcher's shop?

He was chop lifting!